GW00859342

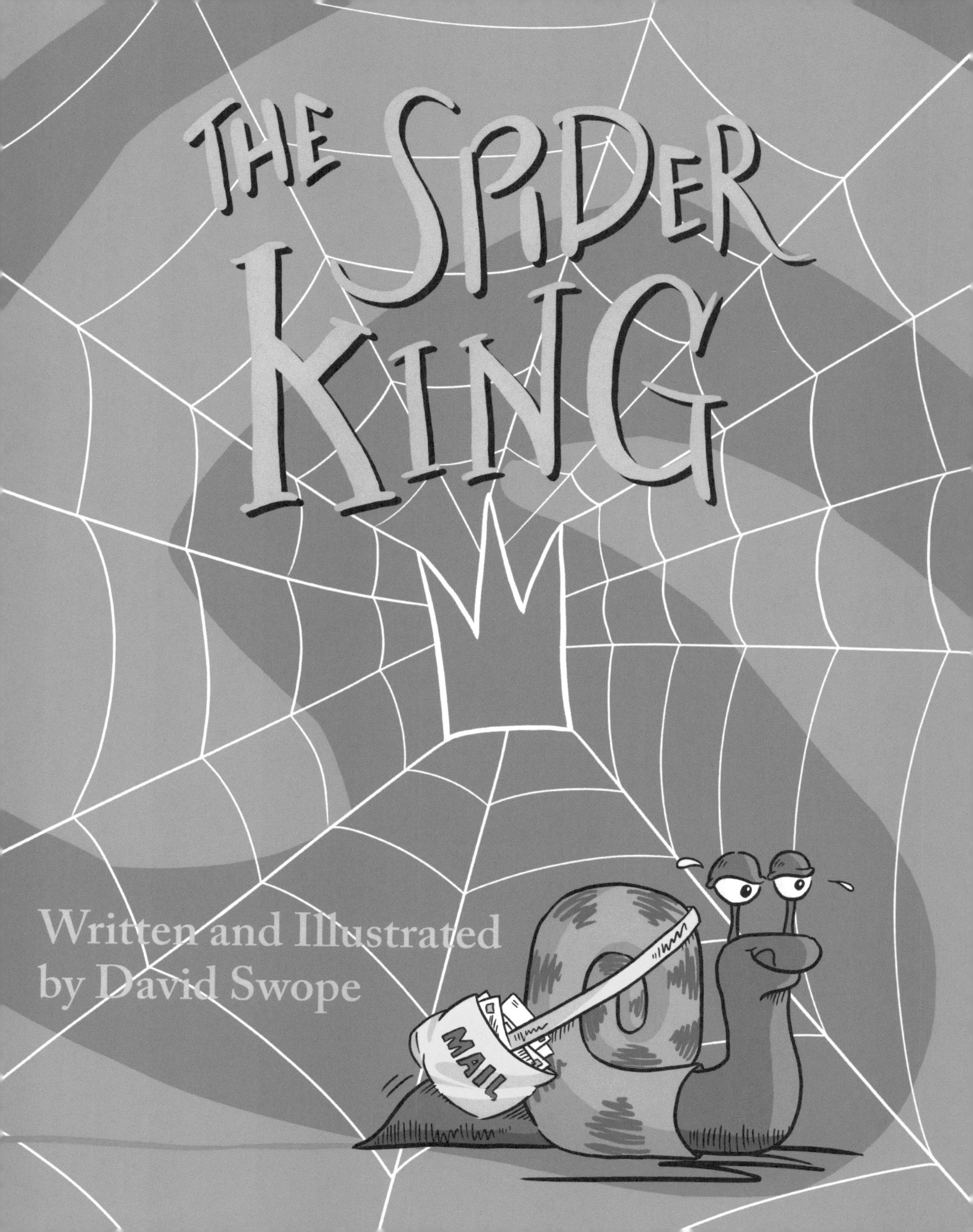
THE SPIDER KING
Written and Illustrated
by David Swope
MAIL

To Jennifer, Ethan and Audrey

Published by Swope Creative
ISBN: 978-0-578-72446-1 (Paperback)
ISBN: 978-0-578-73570-2 (Hardback)

First printing edition 2020

Swope Creative
85 Buckelew St.
Sausalito, CA 94965

SwopeCreative.com

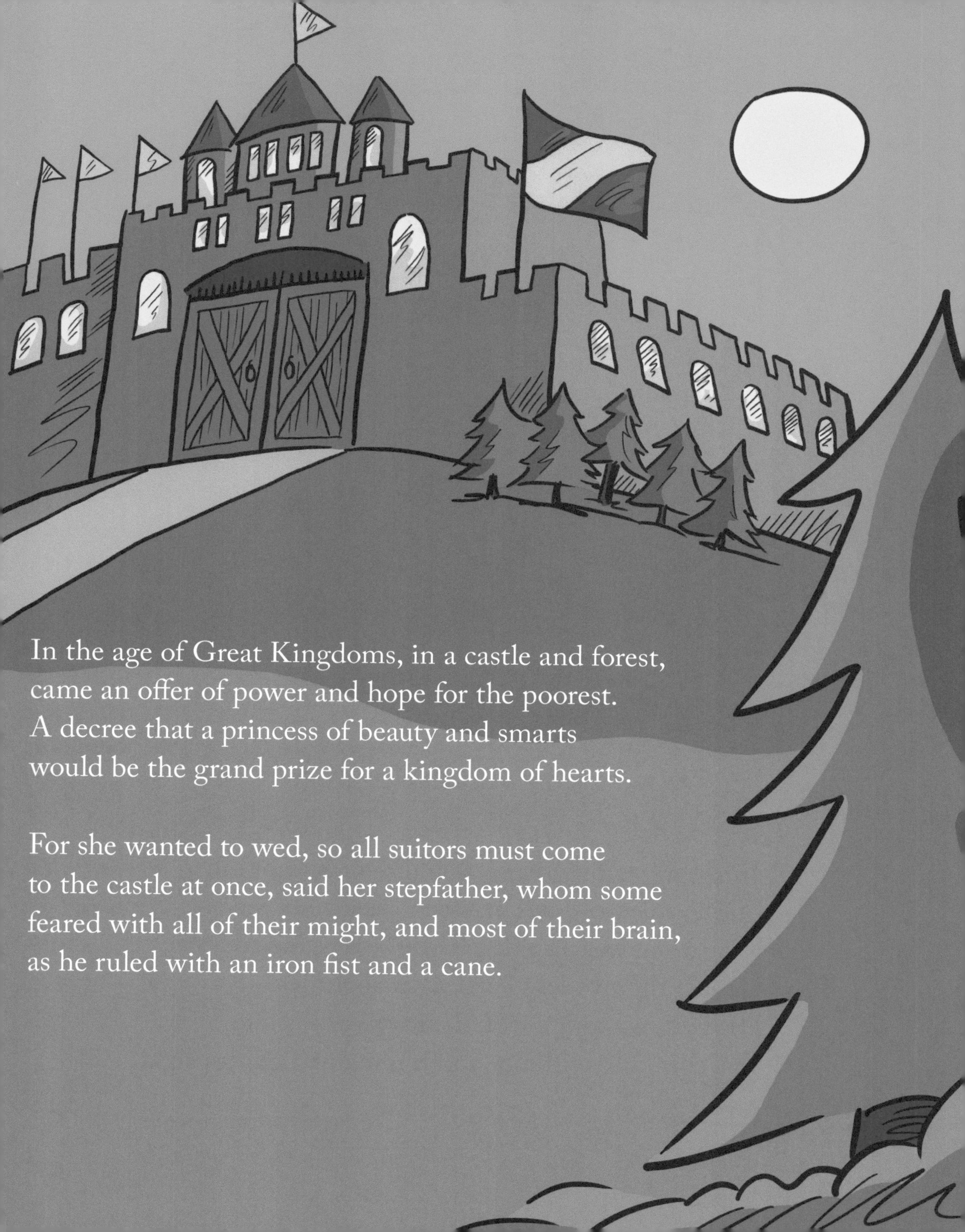

In the age of Great Kingdoms, in a castle and forest,
came an offer of power and hope for the poorest.
A decree that a princess of beauty and smarts
would be the grand prize for a kingdom of hearts.

For she wanted to wed, so all suitors must come
to the castle at once, said her stepfather, whom some
feared with all of their might, and most of their brain,
as he ruled with an iron fist and a cane.

This king, named Fang, you'll see, was not tall.
But he ruled over all between these four walls.
King Fang was a spider, with six legs and four eyes.
He lost the two legs battling dragonflies.
His bark was quite feared, as well as his bite.
Yes, this king with one tooth remained quite a sight.

My daughter, Octavia, a most worthy princess,
shall marry the spider who most impresses
the king, who is me, and here's what you'll get—
the hand of Octavia, and seven more yet.

You shall be part of our royal family,
but first, you have to prove yourself duly.
Show me artistry from your spinnerets.
A masterpiece that no one forgets.

A web that has never been spun anywhere.
Then you will be victor—but one thing beware.
If you don't dazzle with what you've designed,
the punishment shall be *off with your behind!*

Well, that was a threat most spiders would heed.
But Octavia's beauty would surely lead
to a parade of suitors who felt that they would
persuade the king, but if they weren't good,
would depart with no princess, no wedding, no crown.
And the worst pain of all would be just sitting down.

Now, outside the castle, there lived in a shoe
a spider called Louis, or sometimes just Lou.
He lived there alone, always weaving a tale,
like the one where he rode atop a blue whale.
His audience? A carpenter ant, and pet fly,
and a snail who brought mail without fail—by and by.

Young Louis could tell fantastical stories,
spinning his silk into webs of past glories.
He squirted out many fine fabrications.
Who knows if they're true, or prevarications?
So they didn't happen? But maybe they did.
Either way, Louis was one heck of a 'rachnid.

Come gather 'round boys,
and I'll tell you another...
about the king of the castle,
who's really my brother.
Or maybe a cousin,
you see the resemblance?
There's no doubt I'm royal—
a duke or a prince.

Lou, did you hear the word from on high? That Octavia is looking for your kind of guy? I've come from the castle with news of the day. In only two weeks, she'll be given away.
MAIL
Marry her, and you'll be the next Spider King. There's only one problem, just one little thing. A long line of spiders, each with a ring.
But what would she see in a spider like you? You've never done all that you say that you do. She's a princess way up in the castle. If you ask me, this all sounds like a hassle.

Maybe you're right, I'm just Lou from a shoe.
My blood isn't blue. What you say is quite true.
I'm not noble. I'm just spinning my yarns.
I've not been to castles, not even to barns.
The view out this window is all I can see.
But...I'd love to have someone to share it with me.

How long did it take you
to bring us this news?
Have you been traveling
one week—or two?
Well...here is the part
I guess is the worst.
The contest is set
for Tuesday the first.
The first is today!
It's too late for you, Lou.
You're missing your chance,
your dreams won't come true.
MAIL

Stand aside, friends, I've a princess to get.
I've a king to win over. I am not quitting yet.
Fly, I need help, and I'm willing to say,
I'll grant you your freedom. Just hear me, I pray.
Be off to the castle, be quick and be spry.
I need you to be my top-secret spy fly.
Go see what is what, and tell me who's who.
So now that I've cut your leash—*shoo, Fly, shoo.*

Octavia looked out her window that morning
and, with each of her eyes, saw spiders a-courting.
From straight-laced and serious, to foolish or afraid,
could one of these admirers be her true mate?
Dear Father, regarding all of this marrying,
I want a partner who's witty and caring.
Impressive is fine, amazing is great.
But I long to be *laughing* with my soul mate.

Nonsense, Octavia! I have too much money
to leave my inheritance to someone who's funny.
Being king is not easy. It's not to take lightly.
You'll marry the spider who I say is rightly
to sit on the throne with you and abide.
It's time you put all of this joking aside.

And so came the day to award a wedding
to the spider who managed to sway the king.
First, an architect, who did much designing.
He squeezed out a web and spent time refining.

Up next, an accountant, whose web was quite neat.
And a slacker, whose half-baked attempt was no treat.
But when each was done, there was snoozing and snoring.
The roomful of webs was confusing and boring.
The princess did not find these suitors amusing.
And as they were told that they would be losing,
Fang called each to come close, and yelled in his ear...
Take him away—AND OFF WITH HIS REAR!

I'm happy to say, King Fang's in a fit.
Nobody's winning, and now they can't sit.
The king despised all of the webs that were woven.
Lucky for you, no prince has been chosen.
Bad news, I report, is that Weaver, your "pal,"
is up next to win the heart of your gal.

Weaver? Oh no, I must stop that tarantula.
His talent is small, but his ego: *gargantua*.
We used to be friends. There's more to the story—
He copies my webs and gets all the glory.
Weaver's no artist. He hasn't got taste.
That big bug *bugs* me. We've got to make haste!

Hello Your Majesty, or shall I say, "Fang"?
'Cause when you're my in-law, I won't give a dang.
I'll spin the best webs this castle has had.
And I'm looking forward to calling you "Dad."
So stand back and watch a true artist at work...

This guy is beginning to sound like a jerk.
Excuse me?
Who does this spider think that he is—
Michel*ant*gelo? Leonardo da Arachnids?
You haven't seen art from my friend before.
So why not kick this guy right out the door?
My friend here is Lou, and he will show you
a web that is truly splendid, and blow you
away with a magnificent display.
You'll have to agree they should marry today.

Lou? Is that you? Little Lou from the shoe?
Tell me you're not here to try to win too?
I thought that you quit creating your webs
to spend your days talking alone to your pets.
This princess does not want to hear your tall tales.
She doesn't want someone who claims to ride whales.

There's no need to listen to that spider, Weaver. He steals Lou's designs. He's just a deceiver.
I'm sorry, Your Highness, for our interruption. I'll be happy to leave, if you're happy to have *him*.
If this is all true, then prove yourself now. I'll give you a chance, so please show me how Weaver is not all he's cracked up to be, and maybe he shouldn't be marrying me.

With that, the king looked
Louis right in the eye.
And it seemed then to him,
a good time to die.
With everyone watching
for Lou to deliver,
some may have noticed
him starting to quiver.

Octavia leaned in,
and King Fang did too,
waiting to see just
what he would do.

Then Louis did something no spider had done.
It really was simple when it was spun.
He left just one thread from here to right there.
Then Lou stood calmly, while the king glared.

Is that it? *Is that all?*
That's the worst web I've seen!
And then he got mad.
And then he got mean.
HOW DARE YOU COME HERE AND TAKE UP MY TIME!
HOW DARE YOU SPIN JUST THIS ONE LITTLE LINE!

The king waved a leg at the web and it stuck.
He spun, and he twisted, but ran out of luck.
Each turn and each kick from the grumpy old spider
Made that thread wrap him up tighter and tighter.

The room fell silent as they watched the king wriggle.
But the quiet finally broke with a giggle
from Octavia, who laughed when she saw the cocoon
and removed the crown from the wailing buffoon.

It was then she took her new husband in hand.
And in hand and in hand and in hand and in hand.
Thus, Louis gave Octavia the gift she was after.
A lifetime of love, of stories and laughter.
The Spider Queen and her King — happily ever after.